Orphia

Orphia is an only child, it is nearing her sixteenth birthday, she feels a sudden insatiable hunger for knowledge and experience after having a nightmare that she will die young.

'Jacob Bryant's Orphic Egg (1774)'

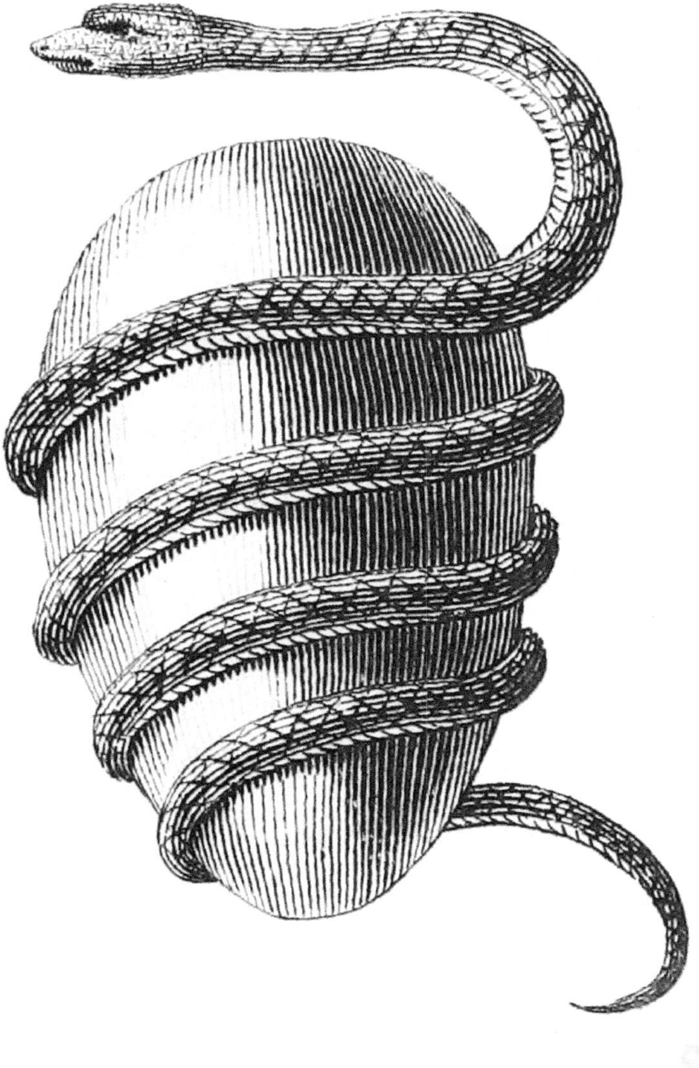

I

The silence was the first thing I noticed. A heavy, suffocating silence that pressed down on me like a physical weight of stone or rock. It was a stark contrast to the cacophony that had just been raging in my mind, a symphony of grief and loss that had left me gasping for air. I lay in bed, tangled in the sheets, my heart hammering against my ribs like a trapped bird. It was indeed too early for anything, especially for facing the lingering images of the nightmare that had wrenched me so violently from slumber.

It wasn't just any nightmare. It was *the* nightmare. The one that had been lurking in the shadows of my subconscious for years, a morbid fascination turned into a terrifyingly vivid reality. It was my own funeral.

I could still see it, feel it, taste the bitter ashes of it in the back of my throat. The church, usually a place of solace and quiet contemplation for those who entered, was filled with a low, mournful hum. I could hear my mothers solemn cries as my casket was carried into view. The air was thick with the scent of lilies, a fragrance I usually found pleasant, now cloying and suffocating. The pews were packed, faces blurred by a veil of tears, yet each one seemed to bore into me with accusatory grief.

Orphia ~

I was there, but I wasn't. I was an invisible observer, floating just above the scene, a ghost at my own wake. I watched as my loved ones filed in, their shoulders slumped with sorrow, their eyes red and swollen. My parents, their faces etched with a pain no parent should ever have to endure, clinging to each other for support. My nieces, trying to be strong, but their forced smiles betrayed the raw grief that threatened to overwhelm them. And then there they were , *them*, *Elijah* and *Beryl* , both strangers to myself at the time of my nightmare , standing at the back, their faces hidden in the shadows, their bodies rigid with a grief that seemed to consume them from the inside out. I longed to reach out, to touch them, to tell them I was okay, but my hands passed right through them. I was a phantom, a whisper in the wind, unseen and unheard.

The service began, the priest's voice a droning monotone that washed over me like a cold, unforgiving wave. He spoke of my life, of my supposed accomplishments, of the potential that had been tragically cut short. But his words felt hollow, inadequate, a pale imitation of the vibrant, messy, imperfect life that I had actually lived.

Then came the eulogies. One by one, people rose to speak, their voices trembling with emotion. They recounted anecdotes, shared memories, painted a picture of me that was both familiar and foreign. They spoke of my laughter, my kindness, my passion, my quirks. But as I listened, a growing sense of unease began to creep into my heart.

Because they were talking about a version of me that no longer existed. Or perhaps, a version of me that had never truly been. They spoke of the woman I could have been, the dreams I could have achieved, the impact I could have made. But they didn't talk about the woman I was, the woman who struggled with bouts of melancholy and self-doubt, the woman who made mistakes and stumbled along the way.

They glorified me, sanitized me, turned me into a saintly figure, devoid of flaws and imperfections. And in that moment, I realized the true horror of the nightmare. It wasn't the thought of death that terrified me. It was the thought of being remembered as someone I wasn't.

The image of my own coffin, draped in flowers, flashed before my eyes. I saw myself lying there, pale and still, a grotesque parody of life. And I knew, with a chilling certainty, that the woman in that coffin was not me. She was a fabrication, a carefully constructed image designed to appease the living.

I woke up then, gasping for air, my body drenched in sweat. The silence of the room was deafening, amplifying the frantic beating of my heart. I stumbled out of bed and made my way to the window, drawn to the faint glimmer of dawn on the horizon.

The world outside was still shrouded in darkness, but I could feel the promise of a new day in the air. A day to breathe, to live, to be imperfectly, authentically me.

I spent the rest of the morning lost in thought, the remnants of the nightmare clinging to me like a shroud. I replayed the faces of my loved ones in my mind, trying to decipher the emotions that flickered across their expressions. Were they truly grieving for me, or were they grieving for the idea of me?

The question haunted me, gnawing at the edges of my soul. I knew that I couldn't control how people remembered me. But I could control how I lived my life, how I treated others, how I presented myself to the world.

And that, I realized, was the key. To live a life that was true to myself, regardless of what others might think or expect. To embrace my flaws and imperfections, to learn from my mistakes, to strive to be a better version of myself each and every day.

Because in the end, all that truly mattered was the legacy I left behind. Not the idealized version of myself that might be eulogized at my funeral, but the real, raw, imperfect human being that I was in life.

As the sun finally broke through the clouds, casting a golden glow over the city, I made a vow to myself. A vow to live each day with intention, with purpose, with authenticity. A vow to be present in the moment, to cherish my loved ones, to embrace the beauty and the pain of life.

The nightmare might return, I knew. But I wouldn't let it define me. I would use it as a reminder to live fully, to love deeply, to be unapologetically myself. Because in the end, that was the only way to truly escape the fear of being forgotten, or worse, of being remembered as someone I wasn't. The best way to prepare for my funeral was to live a life worth remembering, a life that was undeniably, authentically mine. And that was a legacy worth striving for.

2

The ache started subtly, a dull throb deepening in my belly, like a trapped bird beating its wings against the cage of my ribs. I was sprawled on my bed, my breathing almost hoarse. The throbbing grew, spreading outwards, tightening its grip around my abdomen. It was joined by a pull in my legs, a heavy, dragging sensation that made me restless. I shifted, trying to find a comfortable position, but the discomfort persisted, a persistent hum beneath the surface of my concentration.

Finally, curiosity outweighed my fear. I pushed myself up, a groan escaping my dry , cracked lips. It felt like I'd been dragged by my legs across the cold , hard stone floor.

That's when I saw it.

A crimson stain bloomed across the pale blue of my bedsheet, a dark, spreading horror that stole the breath from my lungs. Smaller patches dotted my nightdress, ugly splatters that looked like something had been violently wounded. Panic clawed its way up my throat, choking me. I lifted the sheet higher, my fingers trembling. More blood. So much blood.

My mind raced, a frantic turning wheel of terror. Had I been stabbed? Had something crawled into my bed and attacked me? I had no memory of any injury, no searing pain that would account for this gruesome spectacle. Just the dull ache, now overshadowed by a tidal wave of fear.

My heart hammered against my ribs, a frantic drumbeat echoing the chaos in my head. I felt lightheaded, dizzy, the room beginning to spin. I stumbled off the bed, my legs shaky and unreliable. Each step left a small, horrifying print on the worn wooden floor.

I had to get some help.

"Mother!" The sound tore from my throat, a desperate plea that cracked and splintered in the air. "Mother! Help!"

The silence that followed was agonizing, stretching out like an eternity. I stood frozen, paralyzed by fear and the sheer, inexplicable wrongness of what was happening to me.

Then, the sound of my mother's footsteps, quick and light, came down the hall. Relief washed over me, a fleeting moment of calm in the storm. She would know what to do. She would make it stop.

She burst into the room, her face etched with concern. "What is it? What happened?" Her eyes scanned the room, taking in the overturned chair, the discarded book, the fear etched on my face.

Then her gaze fell on the bed.

Her expression changed, the worry deepening into something I couldn't quite decipher. A flicker of...understanding?...crossed her features before she rushed to my side, her hands gentle as she grasped my shoulders.

"My little dove, what happened? Are you hurt?" She knelt down, her eyes searching mine. "Where does it hurt? Show me."

I couldn't speak, couldn't form the words to explain the inexplicable horror that had taken root in my room, in my body. I just shook my head, tears welling in my eyes.

She followed my gaze downwards, her eyes tracing the bloody path from my nightdress to the stain on the sheet. She gently lifted the hem of my shirt, her fingers probing, searching for a wound.

"Where are you hurt?" she repeated, her voice softer now, laced with a strange kind of tenderness.

I whimpered, shaking my head again. I couldn't tell her. I didn't know what to tell her. All I knew was that something was terribly, terribly wrong.

Then, her fingers brushed against the inside of my thighs. Her movements were hesitant, careful. I flinched, pulling away.

And then, her face changed again. The worry remained, but it was tempered with something else, something knowing, something...inevitable.

She looked up at me, her eyes filled with a mixture of sadness and understanding. “Oh, my dear,” she said, her voice barely a whisper. “It’s okay. You’re not hurt.”

I stared at her, confusion warring with the lingering fear. “But...the blood...” I managed to stammer, the words choking in my throat.

She took a deep breath, her hand still resting gently on my leg. “The blood...it’s coming from between your legs, isn’t it?”

I nodded slowly, shame flooding through me, hot and prickly. I couldn't meet her gaze.

She sighed, a long, drawn-out sound that seemed to carry the weight of centuries. She stood up, pulling me with her, and led me to the edge of the bed.

"Come here," she said, her voice calm and reassuring. "Let me explain."

She sat beside me, her arm around my shoulders, pulling me close. She began to speak, her words soft and measured, explaining the mysteries of the female body, the monthly bleed. The curse that Eve bestowed upon us.

I listened, my mind slowly grappling with the information, the fear gradually receding, replaced by a dawning understanding. It wasn't an injury. It wasn't a monster. It was...natural.

But even as the fear subsided, a different kind of discomfort settled in. A sense of loss, perhaps. The loss of innocence, the loss of the carefree ignorance of childhood. The blood marked a boundary, a crossing over into a new and unfamiliar territory.

My mother's words were comforting, but they couldn't completely erase the initial shock, the visceral terror of seeing that blood. It felt like a violation, an unwelcome intrusion into the safe, predictable landscape of my young life.

"You're becoming a woman," she said finally, her voice filled with a quiet pride.

The words hung in the air, heavy with implication. Becoming a woman. It sounded momentous, important, but also...scary. I wasn't sure I was ready.

She squeezed my shoulder. "Don't be scared," she said, as if reading my thoughts. "It's a big change. A change that should be welcomed with open arms , not tears or fear."

I leaned into her, seeking comfort in her familiar warmth. The blood was still there, a stark reminder of the changes happening within me. But now, it was accompanied by a glimmer of understanding, a flicker of acceptance.

The ache in my stomach and legs hadn't disappeared, but it felt different now, less threatening, more...purposeful. It was the price of admission to a life I hadn't asked to join, a way of living called Womanhood. And as I sat there, covered in blood, with my mother's arms around me, I knew that I was just beginning to understand what that really meant. The fear was still there, a small, persistent voice in the back of my mind, but it was accompanied by something else now, something new, something...hopeful. A hesitant anticipation for the unknown path that lay ahead. The precarious path of becoming a woman.

3

The first yellow lights of dawn were just beginning to paint the sky when I awoke. Not with a start, not with any urgency, but slowly, as if surfacing from a deep, dark ocean. The house was silent, a heavy, muffled silence that pressed down on me. It was the silence of sleeping bodies, of hushed breaths and dreams unknown. A silence my restless spirit could never quite embrace.

I lay there for a long moment, staring up at the faint patterns the burgeoning light cast on my bedroom ceiling. The familiar shapes seemed different somehow, distorted, imbued with a sadness I hadn't noticed before. Was it the light, or was it me? I didn't know. All I knew was that the weight in my chest, the feeling of being adrift, was heavier than usual this morning.

My bare feet made no sound on the wooden floor as I crept out of my room. Each step was deliberate, calculated, a small act of rebellion against the stillness that reigned supreme. The air was cool against my skin, raising goosebumps on my arms. I shivered, drawing my thin cotton nightgown tighter around me.

The house felt vast and empty in the pre-dawn gloom. Shadows danced in the corners of my eyes, playing tricks on my perception. Every creak of the floorboards sent a jolt of fear through me, the fear of being discovered, of shattering the fragile peace. But the fear was a familiar companion, a small price to pay for the solace that I so desperately sought.

My destination was my parents' chambers, a sanctuary I rarely dared to approach. It was a space filled with their secrets, their scents, their lives intertwined. Approaching the closed door, I felt a wave of guilt wash over me, a prickling sensation of trespass. But the longing for what lay beyond the door was a stronger force, a magnetic pull I couldn't resist.

I pressed my ear against the wood, listening for their breathing. The rhythmic rise and fall of their chests was reassuring, a confirmation that they were still lost in the land of dreams. Carefully, I turned the handle, wincing at the faint click it made. The door swung inward, revealing the shadowy interior of their room.

The air inside was thick with the scent of lavender and old books, a peculiar but comforting combination that always reminded me of my mother. The curtains were drawn, but enough light filtered through to illuminate the shapes of the furniture: the heavy oak dresser, the ornate mirrors, the imposing four-poster bed where my parents lay sleeping.

My heart pounded in my chest as I tiptoed towards the dresser. I knew where it was, hidden beneath a small porcelain trinket box my mother kept in the top drawer. *The Key*. The key to my father's library.

He kept it locked, always. Said it was for the protection of the books, some of which were old and delicate. But I suspected there was more to it than that. The library was his domain, his sanctuary, a place where he retreated when the weight of the world became too much to bear. He rarely allowed anyone inside, not even my mother.

But I dreamed of that library. I imagined it as a labyrinth of words, a treasure trove of stories waiting to be discovered. I longed to lose myself in its dusty shelves, to breathe in the scent of aged paper and leather, to trace the spines of forgotten tales.

With trembling fingers, I lifted the trinket box and reached beneath. There it was, a small, tarnished silver key.

I slipped it into my palm, closing my fingers around it as if it were a precious jewel. For me, it was.

The weight of the key in my hand was intoxicating, a promise of untold adventures. But the guilt gnawed at me, a constant reminder of the deception I was perpetrating. I hated the feeling, the sense of being sneaky and dishonest. But the desire to explore my father's library was a powerful drug, one that silenced the voice of my conscience.

I backed out of the room as carefully as I had entered, closing the door behind me with a soft click. I stood there for a moment, listening, making sure my intrusion hadn't disturbed their slumber. Then, I turned and fled, my bare feet silent on the stairs.

The library was at the end of a long, narrow hallway on the second floor. It was a room that held a strange allure for me, even when the door was closed. The dark wood of the door seemed to absorb the light, creating a sense of mystery and intrigue.

As I approached, I could feel my heart pounding in my chest. This was it. This was the moment I had been waiting for. I slipped the key into the lock, my hands shaking so badly I almost dropped it. The lock clicked open with a resounding sound that seemed to echo through the silent house.

I pushed the door open slowly, cautiously, as if afraid of what I might find inside. The air that met me was cool and musty, thick with the scent of old books. It was exactly as I had imagined it.

The room was lined with shelves, floor to ceiling, filled with books of all shapes and sizes. Leather-bound volumes stood shoulder to shoulder with paperbacks, their spines faded and worn. A large mahogany desk sat in the center of the room, cluttered with papers and pens. A single lamp cast a pool of warm light over the desk, illuminating the dust motes dancing in the air.

I stepped inside, closing the door behind me. The silence was even more profound in here, broken only by the faint ticking of a clock in the corner. I took a deep breath, inhaling the scent of the books, allowing it to fill my lungs. It was a comforting scent, a familiar scent, a scent that spoke of knowledge and adventure.

I moved slowly through the room, running my fingers along the spines of the books. I recognized some of them, titles I had seen my father reading. Others were unfamiliar, their titles written in foreign languages. I pulled one down at random, a thick, leather-bound volume with gold lettering on the spine. I opened it to a random page and began to read.

The words were old-fashioned, formal, but they drew me in nonetheless. It was a story of love and loss, of betrayal and redemption. As I read, I forgot about the guilt I had felt, the fear of being discovered. I was lost in the world of the book, transported to another time and place.

I spent hours in the library, lost in the pages of different books. I read poetry, essays, novels, biographies. I devoured words like a starving person, soaking up knowledge and stories like a sponge. The library was a refuge, a sanctuary, a place where I could escape the confines of my own life.

I wasn't looking for anything in particular that day, just wandering aimlessly, letting my fingers trail along the

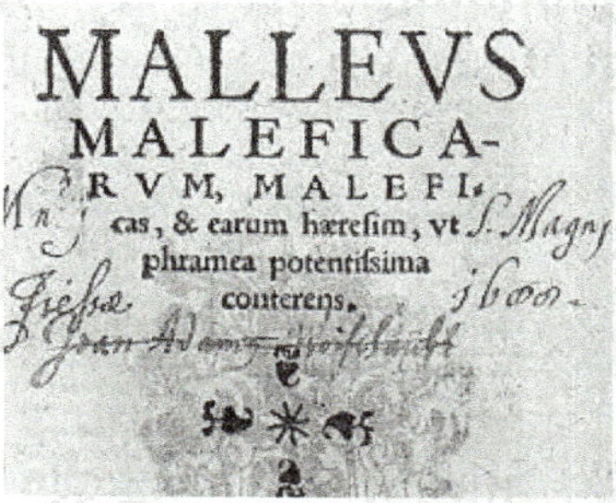

spines, absorbing the silent energy of countless narratives waiting to be rediscovered. I stumbled upon it tucked away in a dimly lit corner, almost hidden behind a stack of crumbling encyclopedias. It was a large, imposing volume bound in dark, almost black leather, its surface cracked and worn with age. The title, embossed in faded gold lettering, sent a shiver down my spine: *Malleus Maleficarum.*

I knew the name, of course. I'd heard stories about witches since I was a child. The leather felt surprisingly smooth beneath my fingertips. As I opened the book, the brittle pages crackled in protest. The paper was thick and yellowed, the ink faded in places, but the text remained surprisingly legible. It was written in Latin, a language I hadn't studied, my father would never allow it , it would be 'of no use' to me, a girl , to know Latin, I only needed to know how to read and write simple letters , but I could make out enough to understand the gist of it.

I expected to be repulsed, to recoil in horror at the descriptions of torture and accusations. And, in part, I was. But there was something else, something that drew me in, a morbid fascination that I couldn't quite explain.

It was the illustrations, grotesque and haunting, that truly captivated me. Woodcuts depicting scenes of supposed witchcraft filled the pages. Women flying on broomsticks, consorting with demons, casting spells under the light of the moon. These weren't just drawings; they were windows into a world of fear, superstition, and repressed desires.

One image, in particular, caught my eye. It depicted a woman tied to a stake, flames licking at her feet. Her face, though crudely rendered, was filled with a mixture of pain and defiance. There was a strange dignity in her posture, a resilience that resonated deep within me. Was she guilty of the crimes she was accused of? Or was she simply a victim of circumstance?

I spent hours poring over the book, lost in its dark and disturbing world. I read about the supposed signs of witchcraft, the methods of interrogation, the justifications for torture. I learned about the witch hunts, the fear of female power and sexuality that lay at the heart of the persecution.

The more I read, the more I felt a strange sense of connection to these women, these outcasts who were branded as witches and condemned to burn. I knew, intellectually, that they were not witches in the way the book described. They were healers, midwives, independent thinkers, women who dared to challenge the norms of society.

And I realise now , men are terribly afraid of women. They know we hold power , that which they do not want to share.

I took the book, feeling a strange sense of responsibility towards it. It wasn't a treasure, not in the traditional sense. It was a reminder of the darkness that lurks within humanity, a cautionary tale about the dangers of fear and ignorance.

Back in my chamber, I placed the *Malleus Maleficarum* under my bed sheet. It was a stark and unsettling presence, but it was also a necessary one.

Sometimes, late at night, when the city is quiet and the only sound is the hum of the animals living in the nearby forest, I would take the book from its hiding place and leaf through its pages. I would look at the illustrations, attempt to read and decipher the Latin text, and think about the women who were condemned by its words. And

I would whisper a silent prayer for them, a prayer for peace and understanding, a prayer that such horrors would never happen again.

I felt a desire , a terrifying hunger to meet one of these witches. From what I had heard , most lived on the outskirts of the village to avoid ever being found.

4

The slam of the front door echoed through the house, a hollow sound that bounced off the familiar floral wallpaper and settled heavily in my chest. He was gone. Another day began , a day of adventure! My father, the local law official, a man of order and unwavering duty, had left for work. He carried with him a sliver of the suffocating silence that had become our constant companion.

I waited, holding my breath, listening for the shift in activity that signaled my mother had started her day. The clatter of pans, the hiss of the gas stove igniting, the rhythmic chop~chop~chop of vegetables being diced ~ a symphony of domesticity playing out in the kitchen, we had courtiers but my mother enjoyed cooking , she would always take part in the preparation of food , I was a world away a large brooding storm raging inside me.

It was my cue.

I crept down the hallway, my bare feet silent on the worn wooden floor. Each step was deliberate, a carefully orchestrated escape. The house held its breath with me, its secrets tucked away in the shadows of dusty furniture and faded photographs. I paused at the living room window, peeking through the gap in the floral curtains. The sun was already high, painting the sleepy town in a warm, golden glow. Everything seemed so normal, so utterly oblivious to the ache in my soul.

My mother was humming now, a tuneless melody that spoke of resilience, of a spirit determined to keep the embers of normalcy flickering. I loved her for it, and I hated it too. It was a constant reminder of what I couldn't be, of the sunny disposition I could no longer muster.

I reached the back door, its paint chipped and peeling, a testament to years of weathering storms. My hand trembled as I reached for the knob, the cold metal a stark contrast to the heat rising in my face. This was it. This was the moment I stepped outside the confines of this house, outside the invisible walls of grief and unspoken words.

The screen door creaked open, a small rebellion against the oppressive silence. The back garden beckoned, a riot of overgrown wildflowers and unruly rose bushes. It was untamed, imperfect, and achingly beautiful. It was a reflection of my own inner landscape.

I stepped onto the dew-kissed grass, the cool moisture seeping between my toes, a small grounding sensation. The air was thick with the scent of honeysuckle and damp earth, a fragrant balm to my troubled mind. I walked past the dilapidated shed, its windows clouded with grime, a silent observer of my solitary wanderings.

I didn't know where I was going, only that I needed to go. I needed to escape the stifling air of the house, the weight of unspoken grief that clung to every corner. I needed to find some semblance of peace, some sliver of solace in the vastness of the world.

I followed the winding path that led through the back garden and into the woods bordering our property. The trees offered a welcome embrace, their leaves rustling in the breeze, whispering secrets I couldn't quite decipher. Sunlight filtered through the canopy, dappling the forest floor in shifting patterns of light and shadow.

Deeper into the woods I went, further away from the house, further away from the memories that haunted me. I stumbled over fallen branches and ducked under low-hanging limbs, the physical exertion a welcome distraction from the turmoil in my head.

I came to a small clearing, a hidden sanctuary bathed in the golden light of the morning sun. A weathered wooden bench sat beneath the shade of an ancient oak tree, a silent invitation to rest. I sank down onto the bench, the rough wood a comforting presence beneath me.

Here, in the heart of the woods, I allowed myself to breathe. I closed my eyes and listened to the symphony of nature – the chirping of crickets, the rustling of leaves, the distant call of a bird. For a brief moment, the weight lifted. For a brief moment, I felt a flicker of something akin to peace.

But the peace was fleeting. The memories lingered, ghosts in the shadows of my mind. The image of his empty chair at the dinner table, the sound of his laughter forever silenced, the gaping hole he had left in our lives.

I knew I couldn't run forever. I knew I would eventually have to return to the house, to the reality and burdens of my life. But for now, in this small clearing, surrounded by the beauty of the woods, I could pretend, just for a little while, that everything was alright. I could pretend that the grief wouldn't consume me. I could pretend that the sun would always shine, even in the darkest of days. And that, I realized, was enough. For now.

5

The dust swirled around my ankles, a gritty caress in the oppressive heat as I creeped towards the village. My pack felt heavier than it had any right to, each meager possession within a lead weight pulling me down.

The village was a cluster of mud-brick buildings huddled together like frightened animals, a stark contrast to the vibrant tapestry of life I'd always known. The air hung thick with the smell of woodsmoke and something else, something indefinable but vaguely unsettling. As I drew closer, the sounds of the village reached me – a cacophony of human activity, a symphony of survival.

People moved with a weary purpose, their faces etched with the lines of hardship. I watched them, each engaged in their own desperate dance of existence. Some were bent double in the fields, their backs glistening with sweat as they coaxed life from the parched earth. Others were foraging in the scrubland surrounding the village, their eyes scanning the barren landscape for anything edible. There was a palpable sense of urgency in their movements, a frantic race against time and dwindling resources.

Near a muddy stream, women knelt on the banks, vigorously scrubbing clothes against rough stones. Their laughter, once a common sound, was now muted, replaced by the weary sigh of resignation. Children, their faces smeared with dirt, chased each other through the narrow alleyways, their games a pale imitation of carefree joy.

Even their laughter held a note of desperation, a plea for normalcy in a world that had turned its back on them.

The aroma of cooking fires mingled with the dust, a tantalizing promise of sustenance that I knew I couldn't afford. I saw a woman stirring a pot over an open flame, her face gaunt and etched with worry. The contents of the pot looked thin and watery, a far cry from the hearty stews I remembered from my mothers cooking. It was a meal born of necessity, a testament to their resilience in the face of scarcity that these people faced.

But it was the figure huddled on the ground that drew my attention the most. An old man, his face a roadmap of wrinkles and hardship, sat with his hand outstretched, his eyes pale with blindness , pleading. He was begging. The sight of it brought a sickly feeling to my stomach. I averted my gaze, ashamed that I had nothing to offer him, that I was barely able to provide for myself at this moment. His silent plea echoed in my own heart, a constant reminder of how far I had fallen.

And then I heard it. A metallic clang, sharp and jarring, cutting through the other sounds of the village. It was a rhythmic, repetitive sound, like metal striking against metal. Curiosity, a dangerous companion in these uncertain times, tugged at me. I needed to know where it was coming from.

Ignoring the ache in my legs, I followed the sound, pushing my way through the bustling crowds. The air grew heavier, the smells more pungent. The aroma of woodsmoke was now overpowered by the metallic tang of blood, a scent that made my stomach churn.

The sound led me to a clearing on the outskirts of the village. What I saw there stopped me in my tracks, a scene of brutal, visceral reality that etched itself into my memory.

A makeshift slaughterhouse had been erected. Chickens squawked and flapped in panicked terror, their feathers flying in all directions. Pigs squealed, their high-pitched cries piercing the air. Men, their faces grim and glistening with sweat , determined, wielded axes and knives with practiced efficiency.

The metallic clang I had heard was the sound of the axe falling, the sound of life being extinguished. Blood flowed freely, staining the ground a dark, crimson red. The air was thick with the scent of death, a suffocating reminder of the harsh realities of survival.

I watched, mesmerized and horrified, as the men worked with a cold detachment, their movements precise and economical. They were not butchers reveling in their task, but rather ordinary people forced to perform a gruesome act to keep their families alive. They were simply trying to survive, just like everyone else in this forgotten corner of the world.

The sight of the slaughtered animals, their lifeless bodies hanging from hooks, sent a wave of nausea through me. These were not just animals; they were sustenance, a desperate measure to stave off starvation. Each death was a victory, a small battle won against the relentless forces of hunger.

I saw a young boy, his face gaunt with malnourishment, no older than ten, watching the slaughter with wide, unblinking eyes. His face was pale, his expression a mixture of fascination and horror. He was learning the harsh lessons of survival, witnessing the brutal reality of where his next meal would come from.

Turning away, I stumbled back towards the village, the image of the slaughterhouse seared into my mind. The metallic clang echoed in my ears, a constant reminder of the fragility of life, the desperation of survival. The faces of the villagers, their weariness and resignation, now seemed to carry a deeper meaning. They were not just surviving;

they were enduring, clinging to life with a tenacity that bordered on madness.

The world I had known, the world of comfort and abundance, seemed a distant, impossible dream. This village, this harsh and unforgiving place, was a reality I had never known.

I found a quiet corner, a place where the dust swirled less fiercely, and sat down, my back against a crumbling wall. The sun beat down mercilessly, but I barely noticed. My mind was still trapped in the slaughterhouse, filled with the cries of the animals, the metallic clang of the axe, the red, crimson stain of blood. It reminded me of my own blood , but that blood shed without injury or death.

I closed my eyes, trying to shut out the horrors I had witnessed, but the images persisted, a haunting reminder of the brutal realities of survival.

As the sun began to dip below the horizon, casting long shadows across the village, I opened my eyes. The villagers were still going about their tasks, their movements slow and deliberate. They were tired, but they were not defeated. They were survivors, and they would continue to fight for their existence, one day at a time.

I took a deep breath, trying to steel myself for the challenges ahead. I didn't know what the future held, but I knew that I could not give up. I had to keep moving, keep searching, keep hoping. For even in this desolate place, in this world of dust and blood, there was still a flicker of hope, a promise of a better tomorrow. And that, I realized, was enough to keep me going.

The forest floor was a tapestry of dying leaves, a muted echo of the vibrant green it once held. A chill wind whispered through the bare branches, a mournful song that seemed to seep into my very bones. I clutched at my bag , its lack of nutrition a heavy weight in my hand, as I trudged deeper into the woods.

Berries. That's what I needed. Something, anything, to ward off the gnawing emptiness in my stomach, a physical manifestation of the larger void within me. It had been hours since I'd last tasted anything substantial.

The air hung thick with the scent of damp earth and decaying wood. It was a smell I knew well, a constant companion in my solitude. I scanned the undergrowth, my eyes searching for the telltale glint of red or blue amongst the brown and grey.

Finally, I spotted them. A small patch of wild blueberries, clinging stubbornly to life on a thorny bush. They were small and tart, not the plump, juicy berries you'd find in a garden, but they were sustenance. A reason to keep going.

My fingers, numb with cold, fumbled with the branches, pricking my skin as I carefully plucked the berries. Each one felt like a small victory, a tiny spark of defiance against the encroaching darkness. I ate a few as I went, the bitter-sweet juice a fleeting comfort on my tongue.

The silence of the forest was broken only by the rustling of leaves and the occasional caw of a crow overhead. It was a lonely sound, a reminder of my isolation. The world outside these woods, with its bustling cities and vibrant life, felt like a distant dream, a world I no longer belonged to.

As the basket slowly filled, a strange sense of tranquility settled over me. The simple act of foraging, of finding sustenance in the barren landscape, was a form of meditation. A way to quiet the demons that haunted my mind.

I knew the berries wouldn't solve my problems. They wouldn't bring back what I had lost, or fill the emptiness that consumed me. But for now, in this quiet corner of the forest, they were enough. They were a reminder that even in the darkest of times, life could still find a way to bloom, however small and fragile. And perhaps, just perhaps, that was enough to keep me going for one more day.

6

The mist clung to the village like a shroud, a damp, grey blanket muffling the sounds of life. I stood at the edge of the familiar, the cobblestones worn smooth by generations of villagers, the thatched roofs hunched low against the encroaching forest.

Why I was leaving, even I couldn't fully articulate. It wasn't hardship, not exactly. The village provided, in its own quiet, unchanging way. It was more a feeling, a persistent gnawing in my gut that the world held more than the predictable rhythm of impoverished life, the endless cycle of planting and harvesting. It was a yearning for something undefined, a whisper carried on the wind that promised adventure, or perhaps just oblivion.

The forest swallowed me whole as soon as I stepped beyond the last cottage. The air, thick with the scent of damp earth and decaying leaves, closed in around me. The sunlight, which had been weak to begin with, was now fractured and diffused, painting the forest floor in a mosaic of shadows.

At first, fear was my constant companion. Every rustle of leaves, every snap of a twig, sent a jolt of adrenaline through me. I imagined eyes watching me from the undergrowth, unseen predators tracking my every move. I gripped the worn handle of my father's old hunting knife, a pathetic defense against the imagined horrors that lurked in the woods.

But as I walked deeper, the fear began to recede, replaced by a strange sense of wonder. The forest was a cathedral of towering trees, their branches intertwined to form a vaulted ceiling. Sunlight streamed through the gaps, illuminating swirling motes of dust and painting the moss-covered trunks in an ethereal glow.

It wasn't long before I encountered my first inhabitants. A pair of deer, a doe and her fawn, stood frozen in a clearing, their large, liquid eyes fixed on me. They were creatures of such delicate beauty, so perfectly adapted to their environment, that I felt like an intruder in their sanctuary. I held my breath, afraid to break the spell, to shatter the moment. Then, with a flick of their white tails, they vanished into the undergrowth, leaving me alone once more.

Later that day, I saw a fox, its fur the color of burnt orange, slinking through the shadows. It moved with a silent grace, its eyes sharp and intelligent. It paused, regarded me with a wary curiosity, and then disappeared as quickly as it had appeared.

These encounters filled me with a strange sense of peace, a feeling of interconnectedness with the natural world. Back in the village, animals were seen as resources, as sources of food and fur. Here, in the heart of the forest, they were something more, something sacred.

As dusk began to settle, painting the sky in hues of purple and grey, I came across a small stream. The water was crystal clear, flowing over smooth, rounded stones. I drank deeply, the cool water quenching my thirst, and then set about building a small fire. The flames crackled and danced, casting flickering shadows on the surrounding trees.

That night, I slept fitfully, the sounds of the forest a constant symphony. Owls hooted in the distance, and the wind whispered through the trees. I dreamt of creatures both real and imagined, of deer with antlers of pure gold, and foxes that spoke in riddles.

The next day, I continued my journey deeper into the woods. I saw wild boar rooting in the undergrowth, their snouts covered in mud. A family of hares darted across my path, their long ears twitching nervously. Each encounter filled me with a sense of awe and respect for the resilience and beauty of life in the forest.

But the forest was not all beauty and tranquility. There was also a darkness, a lurking danger that I could feel in the air. The shadows seemed to deepen, the trees grew gnarled and twisted, and the air hung heavy with an unnatural stillness.

It was in this part of the woods that I saw it ~ the adder , the only poisonous creature in these woods. It lay coiled on a sun-drenched rock, its scales gleaming like polished obsidian. Its eyes, cold and reptilian, fixed on me with an unblinking stare.

I knew, instinctively, that I should not approach. I knew that this creature was deadly, that its venom could bring a swift and agonizing death. But I was drawn to it, fascinated by its beauty and its power.

I stood there, frozen, for what seemed like an eternity, locked in a silent battle of wills. The adder did not move, did not flinch, its gaze unwavering. It was a master of stillness, a patient predator waiting for its opportunity.

Finally, with a supreme effort, I broke the spell. I took a step back, and then another, until I was out of range. The adder remained coiled on its rock, watching me as I retreated.

That encounter shook me to my core. It reminded me that the forest was not a place of idyllic beauty, but a place of constant struggle, of life and death. It reminded me that I was a stranger here, an outsider in a world that was governed by different rules.

As I walked away from the adder, I felt a profound sense of loneliness. The forest, which had once seemed so welcoming, now felt cold and hostile. The creatures I had encountered, which had filled me with such wonder, now seemed menacing and unpredictable.

I realized that I had been somewhat naive, that I had over romanticized the wilderness, that I had failed to appreciate the dangers that lurked beneath its surface. I had come to the forest seeking adventure, seeking escape, but I had found only a deeper understanding of my own vulnerability.

That night, as I huddled around my dwindling fire, I made a decision. I would turn back. I would return home, to the familiar comforts of my room. I had seen the forest, I had experienced its beauty and its danger, and I had learned a valuable lesson about myself.

The journey back was long and arduous, but I walked with a newfound determination. I no longer feared the shadows, no longer imagined predators lurking in the undergrowth. I had faced my fears, and I had survived.

As I emerged from the forest, the village looked different. The cobblestones seemed smoother, the thatched roofs more welcoming. The people I had left behind, who had seemed so ordinary, now seemed like beacons of light in a dark world.

I knew that I would never be the same after my journey into the forest. I had seen things that I could never unsee, I had experienced emotions that I could never forget. But I had also gained something ~ a deeper understanding of myself, and a greater appreciation for the simple comforts of home.

The melancholic ache remained, a quiet reminder of the vastness and mystery of the world beyond the village. But it was an ache tempered with a new found peace, a quiet acceptance of my place in the world. The forest had offered me a glimpse into its soul, and in doing so, had shown me a reflection of my own. And for that, I knew, I would be forever grateful.

7

The front door swung inward before I even reached for the knob, revealing my mother silhouetted against the dim light of the hallway. Her face, usually etched with a weary indifference, was contorted with a rage that felt almost... physical. Before I could even utter a greeting, her hand shot out, a scalding cup of tea splashing across my arm.

The searing pain ripped through me, a shriek escaping my lips before I could stifle it. "You! What have you done?..." she hissed, the rest of her sentence lost in a strangled gasp. I stumbled back, clutching my burning arm, the hot liquid already blistering my skin. I could feel the angry red welts blooming across my flesh.

My father emerged from the shadows, his face pale and drawn, but his eyes, oh, his green eyes blazed with a furious intensity that chilled me to the bone. He wasn't yelling, not yet, but the silence was far more terrifying. He held something behind his back, a glint of polished wood catching the meagre light.

He saw the tea stain on my dress, the fresh burn on my arm, and his fury ignited. He didn't need to ask. He already knew. He knew why I was late. He knew about the missed curfew. He knew about... the book.

"You thief," he spat, the words chilling me more than the tea ever could. He stepped closer, the cane appearing now in his hand, it's dark wood gleaming menacingly. It wasn't a new cane; it was the one he used for his horse, worn and smooth from years of use. But today, it felt like a weapon crafted for pain.

The blows rained down, each one a sharp, searing shock that sent jolts of agony through my body. I didn't cry out; I couldn't. The sobs caught in my throat, choked by a rising tide of despair. I could only curl into myself, trying to make myself small, insignificant, hoping to somehow lessen the force of his rage. The cane whistled through the air, each crack echoing the shattering of my spirit. He didn't stop until the wood felt heavy in his hand, until his own breath was ragged and his body trembled with the aftermath of his outburst.

When it was over, when the silence returned, heavy and suffocating, I lay on the floor, my body bruised and aching, my spirit crushed. The taste of blood mingled with the metallic tang of the air. I felt the lingering heat of the tea burn, a painful counterpoint to the dull ache of the cane blows. My mind raced, replaying the events of the evening, each painful moment etched into my memory. The guilt over the stolen book, the agonizing pain, the overwhelming sense of failure , it all swirled together, threatening to drown me.

Then, my mother was there. She didn't speak, just knelt beside me, her usual harshness gone, replaced by a strange, almost mournful silence. She helped me to my feet, her touch tentative, apologetic. She led me to the bathroom, the familiar smell of soap and disinfectant momentarily distracting me from the throbbing pain.

The water was hot, almost painfully so, but this time it was different. This time it wasn't an instrument of punishment. This time it was a cleansing, a desperate attempt to wash away not just the dirt and the blood, but the shame, the guilt, the crushing weight of their anger. She washed the blood from my skin, her touch gentle but firm, her silence a heavy blanket wrapping itself around me.

As she washed away the physical evidence of their wrath, I felt a different kind of scorching, a slow burn of profound sadness that settled deep in my bones. The physical pain would fade, the bruises would heal, but this feeling, this sense of being perpetually broken, perpetually unworthy, this would remain. The scalding tea, the blows from the cane, were merely the most recent additions to a long catalog of scars that marked my soul. As my mother rinsed the last of the blood from my skin, I knew that the home I'd returned to was not merely a house of bricks and mortar, but a prison of my own making. A prison built of silence, rage, and the enduring weight of unyielding, unforgiving love.

I longed for the forest and the village again , at least there in the mud and leaves I had freedom , my curiosity went unpunished. The feeling of wood and stone under my feet felt harsh and cold, I had neither been welcomed back by my parents nor the building of my birth.

8

The chipped paint on the stained glass windows felt cold against my cheek. Three days. Three days since I'd last tasted freedom, three days of stifling air and whispered anxieties. Three days of pretending. My mother, bless her unsuspecting heart, believed my carefully constructed illness. A raging headache, she'd diagnosed, fueled by the fevered heat emanating, apparently, from my carefully arranged blankets.

I'd perfected the art of deception. The shallow breaths, the pained groans, the strategically placed damp cloth on my forehead , a masterpiece of theatrical suffering. I'd even managed a convincing cough, rattling deep in my chest, a performance worthy of a seasoned actress. But the truth was, I felt nothing but a burning, desperate need to escape. The walls of our manor were closing in, suffocating me with their suffocating love, their stifling concern.

The ruse had worked better than I dared hope. Usually, Mother's watchful eye would pierce through even the most convincing façade. But the exhaustion etched on her face, the worry lines deepening around her eyes , it had clouded her judgment, dulled her instincts. She'd even brought me a bowl of broth, which I'd dramatically pushed aside, murmuring about nausea. My stomach churned, not with sickness, but with a mixture of guilt and exhilaration.

With the sun dipping below the horizon, painting the sky in hues of bruised purple and fading orange, I knew my moment had arrived. Mother was downstairs, humming a mournful tune as she mended a tear in Father's worn hunting jacket. The rhythmic stitch, stitch, stitch provided a comforting backdrop to my escape.

Slowly, painstakingly, I began to unspool my deception. First, a careful loosening of the blankets, then a gentle slide from the bed, my body stiff with apprehension. I felt the familiar sting of guilt, the sharp prick of knowing I was hurting her. But the longing for the forest, for the wild, untamed freedom they offered, outweighed any remorse.

I dressed in the quickest, quietest way possible , a simple shift, worn and comfortable, the only clothes I dared to take. My boots, tucked away beneath the bed, were my silent accomplices. I slipped them on, the leather cool against my skin. One last look at the sleeping form huddled beneath the blankets , a perfect imitation of a sick child , and then I was gone.

The village was quiet, shrouded in the deepening twilight. A few stray dogs barked in the distance, their mournful howls echoing my own restless spirit. I skirted the edges of the cobblestone streets, my heart pounding a rhythm against my ribs. I imagined eyes peering from windows, judging, questioning, but I dared not look back.

The woods beckoned, their shadowy depths promising solace. The familiar scent of damp earth and pine needles filled my lungs, a balm to my restless soul. It was here, amongst the whispering trees and the rustling leaves, that I felt truly alive.

I walked deeper into the forest, the path barely visible beneath my feet. The shadows lengthened, stretching like accusing fingers, but I didn't falter. The moon, a pale disc in the inky sky, cast long, dancing shadows that resembled ghostly figures. They seemed to mimic my own inner turmoil, my own silent struggles.

I found a clearing, a small, secluded space nestled amongst the ancient oaks. The ground was soft, covered in a carpet of fallen leaves. I sank to my knees, the dampness seeping into my shift. I closed my eyes, letting the peace of the woods wash over me.

But the peace was fleeting. Memories flooded back ,the warmth of my mother's embrace, the sound of her laughter, the comforting weight of her hand on my forehead. The guilt gnawed at me, sharper than any physical pain. Was this freedom, or was it simply running away from everything that mattered?

I didn't have the answers. Only the cold kiss of the night air, the rustling leaves, and the gnawing loneliness in my heart. The woods, beautiful and terrifying in their vastness, offered no solutions, only a temporary escape from the painful truth of my own conflicted emotions.

The night stretched on, an endless expanse of darkness and uncertainty. The stars, distant and cold, seemed to reflect the desolation in my soul. And as the first hint of dawn painted the eastern sky, I knew this couldn't last. The woods, once a sanctuary, now felt like a prison , they seemed never ending. The escape was temporary, the longing for home a persistent ache in my heart. I stood, my limbs stiff and aching, and began the long walk back, the silent weight of my choices heavy on my shoulders.

Then I saw them , a young man and a woman splayed out on the grass in the bright moonlight casted into another clearing. The tall trees split apart as though they didn't wish to shroud the two lovers in darkness. I slowly walked towards them , when I finally reached them I nestled down in the grass. The woman's hair was beautiful , black , curly and untamed in the grass. I knew I shouldn't but I reached out and stroked it , I jolted backwards in fear when she opened her bright green eyes. I expected her to look at me with the same stern eyes as my mother or father , but she sat up , her dark hair falling back behind her shoulders , revealing her bosom , she took my hand and placed it in her hair again , let her curls and coils run through my fingers , i traced them down to her chest , I removed my hand for a moment. I had the urge to caress her breasts , as though she had heard my thoughts , she took my hand and placed it gently on her flesh. My heart beat out of my chest as I felt her warm soft skin in my palm. Another urge filled my body , I wanted to suckle , so I brought my mouth to her chest and nursed gently. She sighed gently , running her fingers through my hair. The man next to her began to stir slightly. He captured my attention. I pulled away from the woman and peeked at him through the moonlight. He too had black curls , but he was not awake , I could not see his eyes , at that moment I tried to make guesses as to which colour they might be , brown? Blue? Perhaps even green like his lover?

I was interrupted by my new acquaintance , she gently placed her hand upon my chin , guiding me towards her face , she leaned in closer , I could feel her warm breath brushing against my skin. She brushed her lips against mine , it was an exciting yet somewhat frightening experience , I had no idea how to respond. She slipped her tongue inside my mouth , this made me jump in shock , I pulled away, almost disgusted by her act. She smiled at me and my fear and disgust subsided instantaneously. She layed back down in the tall grass , the pale moonlight hitting her skin , it made her look like a statue , I brought my hand out again running it down her hips and thighs. The hair on her legs was dark but felt so soft in my hands. I was overcome by her beauty. I collapsed on top of her , planting kisses on her neck and collarbone , then down her ribcage , I stopped when my chin collided with the hair between her thighs. I looked back up at her , her green eyes seemed filled with hesitation. I couldn't help myself , I ran my tongue down through the moist warm folds of skin. The unfamiliar taste filled my tongue , it was a strange taste , but yet not unpleasant , I ran my tongue through the folds of skin again. But then I was startled when I heard movement in the grass.

The man was awake standing over me. I fell back in fear , ready to be kicked or beaten , but the man knelt down , placing his fingers on my lips , brushing away some of the liquid from my skin , he placed it in his mouth and smiled at me gently. He ran his fingers through my hair , then leaned in and kissed me on the cheek. They both sat there for a moment gazing at me with an affection that touched my vulnerable soul. Then the both of them slowly removed my dress from my body. When the cold night air hit my skin , I shivered , all the hairs on my body standing upright , but I wasn't cold for too long. The two lovers intertwined themselves with me , their warm welcoming skin brushing against mine.

We laid together in a passionate embrace throughout the night. Finding solace in each other's bodies. I experienced sensations I never felt before and learned things about life that my parents would never bring themselves to educate me on.

When the morning sun shined upon us , we all awoke in unison. Before my two lovers left me we shared each other's names. *Elijah* and *Beryl* the two human beings who gave me a taste of life , who quenched my curiosity beyond all measures. I would have happily died at that moment , fulfilled.

9

The forest floor was a tapestry of decaying leaves, damp and slick under my worn boots. Each step was a sigh, a soft crunch swallowed by the immensity of the woods. The air hung heavy with the scent of pine and damp earth, a fragrance I found comforting. I wandered aimlessly without thought, free from the shackles in my own life, the trees blurring into a green-brown watercolor of beauty.

I hadn't meant to come this deep. The familiar trails of the forest had offered no solace, no escape from the memories that clawed at me. So I'd ventured further, drawn by an innocent curiosity to see what the heart of the woods held. The sun, a forgotten friend, struggled to pierce the canopy, casting long, skeletal shadows that danced around me like restless spirits.

Every rustle of leaves, every snap of a twig underfoot, sent a jolt through me. I was on edge, my senses heightened, as if expecting some unseen force to reach out and claim me. But the forest remained indifferent, a silent observer to my grief.

Hours must have passed. The light began to fade, painting the sky in hues of bruised purple and somber grey. I stumbled, more than walked now, my legs heavy with exhaustion, both physical and emotional. Just as I considered turning back, a sound stopped me dead in my tracks.

A whimper.

It was a low, guttural sound, laced with pain and fear. It cut through the silence, resonating with the hollowness inside me. I hesitated, my first instinct to flee. But something held me back. A flicker of empathy, perhaps, or maybe just a morbid fascination with another creature's suffering.

I followed the sound, pushing through thickets of thorny bushes, my heart pounding in my chest. The whimper grew louder, leading me deeper into the increasingly oppressive gloom. And then I saw him.

A stag.

He was magnificent, even in his suffering. His antlers, a crown of polished bone, were tangled in a web of branches. One of his hind legs was twisted at an unnatural angle, and a dark stain bloomed on his flank. He lay on his side, his breath coming in ragged gasps, his eyes wide with pain and terror.

He flinched as I approached, his muscles tensing. I stopped, holding up my hands in a gesture of peace. "It's okay," I whispered, my voice trembling. "I won't hurt you."

He didn't understand, of course. He only saw a potential threat, another reason to fear. But something in my voice, perhaps the shared pain, seemed to calm him slightly. He stopped struggling, his gaze fixed on me, his breath still ragged.

I knelt beside him, keeping a safe distance, and assessed the situation. The leg was clearly broken, and the wound on his flank looked deep and infected. There was nothing I could do. I had no tools, no medical knowledge, nothing to offer him but my presence.

A wave of helplessness washed over me, mirroring the despair that had been consuming me for weeks. I wanted to fix him, to ease his pain, but I was powerless. Just like I had been powerless to prevent the tragedy that had shattered my life.

Tears welled up in my eyes, blurring my vision. I reached out slowly, cautiously, and rested my hand on his velvet-soft nose. He flinched again, but this time, he didn't pull away.

"I'm so sorry," I whispered, my voice thick with emotion. "I wish I could help you."

He closed his eyes for a moment, and I felt a tremor run through his body. Whether it was from pain or something else, I couldn't tell. But in that moment, I felt a connection, a shared understanding of what it meant to suffer.

I stayed with him as the darkness deepened, the forest growing ever more silent. I stroked his nose, whispering words of comfort, though I knew he couldn't understand. I told him about my pain, about the loss that had left me hollow, about the emptiness that threatened to consume me.

And as I spoke, something shifted within me. The act of comforting him, of acknowledging his suffering, somehow eased my own. It was as if his pain was a mirror, reflecting my own back at me, forcing me to confront it, to acknowledge it, to accept it.

The stag's breathing grew shallower, his body weaker. I knew his time was near. I continued to stroke him, whispering softly, until his breath finally stilled. His body lay still, heavy against the forest floor.

I stayed with him for a long time, long after the moon had risen, casting its silvery light through the trees. I felt a strange sense of peace, a quiet acceptance that I hadn't felt in weeks.

He was gone. But in his passing, he had given me something. A reminder that even in the darkest of times, there is still beauty, still connection, still the possibility of comfort.

I stood up, my legs stiff and aching. The forest felt different now, less menacing, more accepting. I turned and walked back the way I had come, my steps lighter, my heart a little less heavy.

The path back was long and arduous, but I didn't mind. I knew I had a long way to go before I could truly heal, before I could fully embrace life again. But I also knew that I wasn't alone. I carried the memory of the stag with me, a reminder that even in the face of death, there is still life, still hope, still the possibility of finding solace in the most unexpected places.

The forest floor remained a tapestry of decaying leaves, but now, I saw it differently. I saw not just decay and death, but also the promise of new beginnings, the cycle of life and death that continues, endlessly, regardless of our individual sorrows. And in that understanding, I found a flicker of hope, a tiny spark of light in the darkness. It wouldn't magically erase the pain, but it was enough to keep me moving forward, one step at a time, into the dawn. The memory of the stag, his pain, and the quiet dignity of his passing, would stay with me always, a gentle reminder to cherish the beauty of life, even in the face of unimaginable loss.

The air grew heavy, thick with the scent of pine and something else, something acrid and unsettling. A prickling sensation crawled across the back of my neck. I glanced behind me, but saw only the deepening gloom between the trees. Just the shadows playing tricks, I told myself, but the feeling persisted, a cold knot tightening in my stomach.

I quickened my pace, half-running now, the silence amplifying every rustle in the undergrowth. Then, a flicker of movement. A flash of color , the dull brown of homespun cloth , just beyond the gnarled trunk of an ancient oak. I stopped, my breath catching in my throat.

"Hello?" My voice was a thin, reedy sound, swallowed by the vastness of the woods. There was no reply, only the rustling of leaves, perhaps magnified by my own fear.

I started walking again, more cautiously this time, my eyes constantly scanning the periphery. And then I saw him. Just a glimpse, a fleeting impression burned into my retina. A figure, gaunt and cloaked in shadow, mirroring my movements, keeping pace just beyond the treeline.

It was Elias, the baker's son. I remembered him well enough, a quiet, unassuming boy, always with flour dusting his eyelashes. Why was he following me?

A wave of nausea washed over me. I felt vulnerable under the watchful view of this young man. Why was he following me?

He kept his distance, always just out of reach, a silent, watchful presence. I couldn't outrun him. I wouldn't even try. This chase, this silent accusation, was my penance. I was trapped, not just by the trees, but by the heavy weight of my own guilt. And as the last sliver of sun bled from the sky, I knew I was being led, inevitably, towards a reckoning I couldn't escape.

When we finally reached the edge of the woods , I stopped and turned. Elias was now only a couple metres behind me.

"Young Lady , may I escort you back to your dwelling? Tis not proper for you to be out alone in these woods"

He was not asking me a question , I knew well enough to know that. My second adventure had ended , been cut short even, I looked away from him in absolute defeat , rolling my eyes back into my skull. *For heaven's sake!*

10

The dust motes danced in the single shaft of sunlight that pierced the gloom of the attic, illuminating the air like tiny, frantic stars. I watched them, mesmerized, as the throbbing in my legs slowly ebbed, leaving behind a dull, persistent ache that resonated with the hollowness in my chest. They were beautiful, those insignificant particles, free to drift wherever the unseen currents carried them. A freedom I craved with every fiber of my being.

It had been foolish, I knew, to think I could actually escape. This wasn't the first time, after all. Each attempt, fueled by a desperate yearning for something beyond the suffocating confines of our house, ended the same way: with the heavy dread of anticipation, followed by the brutal, inevitable punishment.

The cane itself was a monstrous thing, thick and gnarled, its polished surface gleaming with a sinister sheen. It hung on a hook near the hallway door, a constant, silent threat. I could almost feel its weight in my hand, the way its smooth surface would press against my palm before descending with terrifying force.

The memory of the afternoon was already blurring at the edges, the details dissolving into a swirling vortex of terror and pain. I had been halfway to the town, my small bag clutched tight, the taste of freedom already sweet on my tongue. But then, he found me. His face, usually impassive, was contorted with a rage I had only glimpsed before. He hadn't said a word, just grabbed my arm with a grip that made me gasp, and dragged me back home.

The beating... I flinched, even now, at the recollection. The first strike had taken my breath away, a searing pain that ripped through my muscles and bone. I had cried out, a strangled sob that was swallowed by the thick, oppressive silence of the house. Each subsequent blow was a fresh wave of agony, each one chipping away at my resolve, leaving me breathless and trembling.

Mother had tried to stop him, I remembered that. Her voice, usually soft and comforting, rising in a desperate plea. "Please, Thomas, that's enough! You'll kill her!"

But he had been beyond reason, his eyes glazed with a frightening intensity. He pushed her away, a rough shove that sent her stumbling against the wall. The look on her face, a mixture of fear and heartbroken resignation, was almost as painful as the blows themselves. She knew, just as I did, that there was no reasoning with him when he was like this.

Finally, it had stopped. The silence that followed was almost worse than the pain, punctuated only by my ragged breathing and the soft whimpers that escaped my lips. He had stood over me, his chest heaving, the cane still clutched in his hand. He didn't say a word, just looked at me with an expression I couldn't decipher, a mixture of anger, disappointment, and something else... something that looked almost like pity.

Then, he had dragged me to my room. A small, usually comforting space that had become my prison. He slammed the door shut and locked it. The click of the lock echoed in the silence, a definitive sound that sealed my fate.

That was two days ago. Two days without food, without water, without a single word or gesture of comfort. The hunger was a gnawing, persistent ache in my stomach, a constant reminder of my transgression. My throat was parched, my lips cracked and bleeding. I had licked them raw in a futile attempt to find some moisture.

But the physical discomfort was nothing compared to the crushing weight of loneliness. The silence was deafening, broken only by the occasional creaks and groans of the old house, sounds that only amplified my isolation. I pressed my ear against the door, listening for any sign of life, any indication that I hadn't been completely forgotten. But there was nothing.

I thought of Mother, and a fresh wave of despair washed over me. Was she alright? Had he hurt her? I imagined her sitting downstairs, her face etched with worry, her heart breaking for me. I longed to hear her voice, to feel her gentle touch, to know that I wasn't entirely alone in the world.

I had tried everything to escape. I had rattled the doorknob, kicked at the door, even tried to pry open the window with a hairpin. But it was no use. The door was solid, the window sealed shut with thick, ancient putty. I was trapped.

As the hours stretched into days, a strange sense of detachment began to creep over me. The pain, both physical and emotional, seemed to recede, replaced by a hollow emptiness. I spent my time staring at the ceiling, tracing the patterns of the water stains, lost in a world of my own creation.

The dust motes still danced in the sunlight, but now they seemed less like symbols of freedom and more like mocking reminders of my own captivity. I imagined them laughing at me, pitying my weakness.

I knew, deep down, that I couldn't keep running away. It only led to pain, to disappointment, to the inevitable return to this suffocating existence. But the thought of resignation, of accepting my fate, was almost as unbearable as the beatings.

What else was there to do but dream? To dream of a different life, a different world, a place where I could be free to choose my own destiny. A place where the dust motes danced not in the gloom of an attic, but in the open air, carried by the gentle breeze to far-off, unknown lands. And maybe, just maybe, one day, I would find a way to follow them. The hope, fragile and flickering as it was, was the only thing that kept me going. It was the only thing that kept me alive.

As hours passed by my thoughts began to grow a seed of hatred. I thought , when they finally let me out I would kill them both! Slit the soft pale skin of their throats! Then and only then could I truly be free , an orphan , a child all alone , but at the very least without chains around my wrists and ankles that dig into my skin making my blood pool upon the floor.

But then I thought about what their screams would sound like , how the blood would spit out violently from their bodies onto their clothes , onto the cold stone floor! How would I clean it? Where would I bury their bodies? I most certainly could not give them a funeral. There would be no mercy in it!

Why was I born a woman? Why did God have such resentment towards me to give me Eve's curse? What made me unworthy of a masculine life , one where I could live as I please , where I would be taught how to read and write whatever I like , how to hunt , have authority and power. But the lord chose for me to be a woman! Why did he create us? What is the purpose exactly , to just bare children? How cruel , how *Unforgivable!*

II

The door, a formidable slab of oak, unyielded after weeks of resistance. I hadn't seen the sun, tasted fresh air, or heard voices beyond the echoing pronouncements delivered through the crack at the bottom. My world had shrunk to the dimensions of four walls, a bed, and the gnawing silence of my own thoughts. Then, the click. A sound sharp and final, like the snapping of a bone.

Blinking against the sudden influx of light, I saw him. My father. His face, etched with lines I hadn't noticed before, was a battlefield of conflicting emotions: relief, apprehension, and a deep, unwavering sadness. He didn't speak, just held out his hand. It was a gesture I once would have welcomed, a symbol of comfort and protection. Now, it felt like a brand, a reminder of the chasm that had grown between us.

He led me out, not gently, but with a firm hand on my arm, steering me through the house. The familiar surroundings felt alien, distorted by the weeks of isolation. The scent of lavender polish and beeswax, once comforting, now felt cloying, suffocating. My feet dragged, heavy with resentment and a strange, burgeoning defiance.

Outside, the air was crisp and carried the scent of damp earth and dying leaves. The world was vibrant, teeming with life, but I felt disconnected, an observer rather than a participant. People averted their eyes as we passed, whispering behind cupped hands. I was a spectacle, a curiosity, the girl who had gone mad.

The ride in the carriage was silent, the tension thick enough to choke on. My father stared straight ahead, his knuckles white on the door's wooden handle. My mother averted her eyes from my watchful gaze. I watched the landscape blur past, a kaleidoscope of spring hues. The vibrant colours felt like a mockery of my inner turmoil, a stark contrast to the bleakness that had taken root within me.

We arrived at the church. Its imposing façade, built of grey stone and stained glass, loomed against the sky. The spire, a beacon of faith for so many, felt to me like a sharpened point, aimed directly at my beating heart. This was his answer, the place he thought would heal me, would exorcise the demons that had taken hold.

He ushered me inside, into the cavernous space filled with the hushed murmur of voices and the heavy scent of incense. The air was thick with piety, a suffocating blanket of reverence that made my irritated skin crawl. Rows of polished pews stretched before me, filled with familiar faces, their expressions a mixture of pity and apprehension.

My father guided me to a seat near the front, close enough to the altar that I could almost reach out and touch the gold-plated cross. He knelt beside me, his head bowed in prayer. I remained standing, rigid and defiant, my gaze fixed on the priest who stood before the congregation, droning on about forgiveness and redemption.

He was a man I had known all my life, a man I had once respected. Now, his words felt hollow, empty platitudes offered to appease a God I no longer believed in. A surge of anger, hot and visceral, rose within me, threatening to erupt.

As he raised the chalice, his voice booming through the sanctuary, I could no longer contain myself. I spat. The saliva landed squarely on his pristine white robes, a blatant act of desecration that silenced the room completely. Gasps rippled through the congregation, heads turned, eyes widened in shock and horror.

My father recoiled, his face a mask of disbelief and shame. He tried to pull me down, to silence me, but I pushed him away, my voice rising above the stunned silence.

"Lies!" I screamed, my voice raw with fury. "All of it is lies! You preach love and forgiveness, but where was God when I needed him? Where was he when my world fell apart?"

I lunged towards the altar, my hands sweeping across the surface, knocking over candlesticks and sending them crashing to the floor. Wax dripped onto the carpet, mingling with the metallic scent of blood from the cuts on my hands.

"He's not real!" I shrieked, my voice cracking with emotion. "He's a figment of your pathetic imaginations, a crutch for the weak! You waste your lives praying to a phantom, while the world crumbles around you!"

The priest stood frozen, his face pale with shock. People were scrambling back, their faces contorted with fear and disgust. The sanctuary, once a place of peace and reverence, had become a scene of chaos and sacrilege.

My father, his face a mask of agro and nervousness, tried to reason with me, to calm me down. But his words were lost in the storm of my rage. I was beyond reason, consumed by a darkness that had taken root deep within my soul.

"You all worship a tyrant!" I screamed, my voice hoarse. "A cruel and capricious God who delights in suffering! He demands your obedience, your sacrifice, but offers nothing in return!"

I continued my tirade, a torrent of blasphemous pronouncements that echoed through the sanctuary. I cursed God, I cursed the church, I cursed the blind faith that had held these people captive for so long.

My father, desperate to stop me, lunged forward and grabbed me, his arms wrapping around me in a tight embrace. I fought him, kicking and screaming at the top of my lungs, but he was stronger than me. He held me tight, whispering pleas in my ear, begging me to stop.

But I wouldn't stop. I couldn't stop. The words poured out of me, a venomous stream of anger and despair. I was a broken vessel, spilling my pain onto the world.

Then, everything went black.

I don't remember the blow, the moment of impact. All I remember is the searing pain in my head and then, nothing. Just a void, a silent oblivion that swallowed me whole.

I woke up in my room, the same four walls that had been my prison for days. The only difference was the throbbing pain in my head and the lingering taste of bile in my mouth. The memory of the church, the sacrilege, the rage, was a jumbled mess, a nightmare that clung to the edges of my consciousness.

My father was sitting in a chair beside my bed, his face etched with exhaustion and sorrow. He didn't speak, just watched me with hatred growing in his eyes.

I knew what he had done. He had silenced me, the only way he knew how. He had used force to subdue me, to quell the rebellion that had threatened to tear us apart.

And in that moment, lying in my bed, surrounded by the familiar confines of my prison, I felt a profound sense of defeat. I had lost. The darkness had won. And I was left alone, with nothing but the echoing silence of my own shattered soul. The church bells in the distance began to ring, a mournful peal that seemed to mock my despair. The day, once filled with such promise, now felt like a tomb. A tomb where my spirit was buried alive.

12

My entrapment had started to affect my body , I awoke every morning nauseous and weak , releasing vomit into my chamber pot. As days of this sickness turned into weeks my mother seemed to grow more and more fearful. I told her "Mother , just let me die , let me go" , but my words did not seem to trouble her? She assured me that I was not going to die. Did she know something that I did not?

****

The chill had settled deep into my bones, a permanent resident it seemed, much like the sorrow that clung to me these last few months. The fire in the hearth sputtered weakly, casting dancing shadows that mocked my stillness. I hadn't the strength to coax it into a proper blaze, nor the inclination. What was the point? Warmth couldn't penetrate the icy grip that had taken hold of my very soul.

The knocker on the door was a sharp, unwelcome intrusion. I hadn't seen anyone in weeks, I hadn't wanted to. The world outside felt distant, unreal, as though separated from me by a thick pane of glass. Each day was a gray, indistinguishable blur, marked only by the slow, agonizing crawl towards nightfall.

The door creaked open, admitting a gust of wind and a figure cloaked in dark wool. It was Doctor Ainsworth, his face etched with concern beneath the brim of his hat. He was a kind man, in his way, though his medicine always seemed a desperate gamble against the unseen forces that plagued us all. My mother stood behind him , her eyes wide with anticipation.

"Orphia," he said, his voice low and gentle. "How are you feeling?"

The question hung in the air, heavy with unspoken understanding. How was I feeling? Like a ship adrift at sea, lost in a fog so thick I couldn't even remember the last time I saw the shore.

"Not any good," I managed, waving a listless hand towards the meager fire. "Just... weary."

He nodded slowly, his eyes scanning the room, taking in the dust motes dancing in the weak sunlight, the unwashed dishes stacked precariously on the table, the overall air of neglect that permeated everything. He knew. He always knew.

He set down his bag on the worn rug and approached me, his gait slow and deliberate. "May I examine you, Orphia?"

I offered him a weak smile, the effort of it feeling like lifting a great weight. "If you think it will do any good."

He pulled up a stool and sat beside me, his touch surprisingly warm as he took my wrist, his fingers pressing against the delicate pulse point. He held it there for a long moment, his brow furrowed in concentration. Then, he moved to my forehead, his hand cool against my skin. He peered into my eyes, examining the color of my tongue, asking questions that I answered with monosyllabic replies.

The examination felt intrusive, yet somehow comforting. It was a human connection, a small thread tethering me to the land of the living. When he was finished, Dr. Ainsworth sighed, a sound that seemed to carry the weight of centuries of medical uncertainty.

"Your humors are out of balance, Orphia," he pronounced, his voice grave.

The humors. Blood, phlegm, yellow bile, and black bile. The cornerstones of health, the delicate forces that, when properly aligned, ensured a life of vigor and vitality. But when they fell into disharmony, as they clearly had with me, the result was sickness, both physical and emotional.

"Too much black bile, I suspect," he continued, confirming my own silent diagnosis. "Melancholy. It weighs heavily upon the soul, does it not?"

I nodded, tears pricking at my eyes. He understood the suffocating darkness that had enveloped me, the crushing weight of grief that had settled upon my chest. It was as though a part of me had died with the end of my childhood near, leaving behind an empty shell filled only with sorrow.

"Your coming of age has taken a toll on you," he said softly, his gaze filled with compassion. "But you cannot allow melancholy to consume you, Orphia. It will steal your life away, piece by piece."

Easier said than done, I thought bitterly.

"I have a treatment," he said, reaching into his bag. "I believe it will help restore balance to your humors."

He produced a small, leather-bound case, and from it, he extracted a gleaming array of instruments: a tourniquet, a bowl, and a small, wickedly sharp lancet. My heart lurched in my chest.

"Bloodletting?" I asked, my voice barely a whisper.

He nodded. "It is a time-honored practice, Orphia. By removing some of the excess blood, we will be releasing the black bile that is poisoning your spirit. It will cleanse you, both physically and emotionally."

I stared at the lancet, its polished surface reflecting the firelight in a malevolent gleam. The thought of it piercing my skin, drawing forth my lifeblood, filled me with a primal fear. But the thought of continuing to live in this suffocating darkness was even more terrifying.

"Are you sure it is necessary?" I asked, clinging to a last shred of hope.

He hesitated for a moment, his eyes filled with uncertainty. "It is my best judgment, Orphia. I believe it will help you."

I looked at his face, searching for any sign of doubt, but I saw only concern and a deep-seated belief in the efficacy of his craft. And perhaps, just perhaps, he was right. Perhaps this drastic measure was the only way to break free from the shackles of grief.

"Very well," I said, my voice resigned. "Do what you must."

He nodded, his movements now swift and purposeful. He tied the tourniquet tightly around my arm, the pressure making my veins swell. He swabbed the inside of my elbow with a cloth, then took the lancet in his hand.

"This will be painful," he warned.

I closed my eyes, bracing myself for the pain. The prick of the lancet was sharp and immediate, followed by a warm, flowing sensation as my blood began to seep into the bowl. I opened my eyes and watched, mesmerized, as the dark, viscous liquid filled the bottom of the container.

Doctor Ainsworth continued to draw blood, his face impassive. I felt a strange sense of detachment, as though I were watching this scene unfold from a great distance. The room began to swim, and a wave of dizziness washed over me.

"Enough," I gasped, my voice weak. "I... I can't..."

He immediately released the tourniquet and applied a clean cloth to the wound. "You are losing too much blood," he said, his voice filled with concern.

He bandaged my arm and helped me lie down on the worn couch. I closed my eyes, feeling weak and drained, but strangely... lighter. As though a weight had been lifted from my chest.

Doctor Ainsworth sat beside me, monitoring my pulse. "Rest now, Orphia," he said softly. "Let the treatment take hold in the body."

I drifted off to sleep, my dreams filled with swirling images of blood and darkness, of a stranger's smiling face and the cold, empty sea. When I awoke, the sun was setting, casting long shadows across the room. Doctor Ainsworth was gone, but a small vial of herbs sat on the table beside me.

"For your nerves," a note read.

I sat up slowly, feeling weak but... different. The suffocating darkness hadn't entirely lifted, but it felt... thinner. As though a crack had appeared in the wall that had been holding me captive.

Whether it was the bloodletting, the herbs, or simply the passage of time, I couldn't say. But for the first time in months, I felt a flicker of hope. A tiny spark in the darkness.

The road ahead would be long and difficult, I knew. The pain of loss would always be with me. But perhaps, just perhaps, I could find a way to live with it. To carry the memory of my adventures with me, not as a burden, but as a flame to light my way. Maybe, just maybe, I could find my way back to the shore.

13

The light was a dull ache behind my eyelids, a persistent throb that dragged me from the murky depths of sleep. It wasn't the vibrant, hopeful light of a new morning, but a muted, greyish thing that seemed to seep into my bones, mirroring the dull ache that had become my constant companion. I blinked, the world swimming into focus in hesitant fragments. The peeling wallpaper, the chipped paint on the window frame, the familiar floral pattern of the quilt pulled up to my chin , these were the landmarks of my small, suffocating world.

Then I saw her.

My mother sat in the armchair beside my bed, a silent sentinel bathed in the same melancholic light. Her head was bowed, her thin, graying hair falling forward to obscure her face. In her hands, she held a worn, leather-bound book, its pages thin and brittle with age. The Bible.

The sight of it sent a fresh wave of weariness through me. Not because of the book itself, but because of what it represented , a desperate plea, a silent bargaining chip held out to a God who seemed deaf to our prayers.

She read the passages aloud:

"Praise the Lord, my soul, and forget not all his benefits ~ who forgives all your sins and heals all your diseases."

My throat felt scratchy and raw as I tried to speak. "Mother?" I croaked, the sound barely audible above the ticking of the cold wind in the hallway.

She startled, her head snapping up, her eyes widening behind her spectacles. A flicker of something – relief, perhaps, or maybe just plain exhaustion crossed her face before settling back into the usual worry lines.

"Oh, little dove, you're awake." Her voice was soft, a little raspy. She closed the Bible, placing it gently on the small table beside her. The sound of the worn leather against the wood seemed amplified in the quiet room. "I didn't mean to wake you."

"What were you doing?" I asked, the words still catching in my throat. "Reading?"

She hesitated, her gaze drifting back to the Bible as if drawn by an invisible thread. "Just... saying a few prayers, my love."

I knew better. My mother didn't just "say a few prayers." She wrestled with God, pleaded with Him, bargained with Him, all in the hopes of a miracle that never seemed to come. I knew because I had heard her, night after night, her whispered supplications, a constant hum in the background of my own pain.

"For me?" I asked, the question hanging heavy in the air.

She reached for my hand, her fingers surprisingly strong despite her frail appearance. They were rough, calloused from years of hard work and worry. "Always for you, darling."

Her touch was warm, comforting, but even that couldn't penetrate the chilling dread that had taken root in my heart. I knew what was coming. I had seen it in her eyes, in the forced cheerfulness of her smile, in the way she lingered a little too long at my bedside.

"You know," she said, her voice taking on a lighter, almost airy quality, "your sixteenth birthday is just around the corner."

My breath hitched. The words hung in the air, shimmering with unspoken anxieties. Sixteen. A milestone, a mark of passage, a promise of possibilities. For most girls, it was a time of finding suitors , marriage and moving out of home. For me, it felt like a looming precipice.

"A couple of days," I managed to say, my voice barely a whisper.

She squeezed my hand. "That's right. Just a couple of days. And I'm praying, darling , praying with all my might, that you'll be feeling better by then."

The words were like a punch to the gut. Praying that I'd be better. Not wishing, not hoping, but praying. As if my fate hung precariously in the balance, dependent on the whims of a higher power. As if my own body, my own will, had no say in the matter.

I looked at her, at the hope flickering in her tired eyes, and a wave of guilt washed over me. Guilt for being a burden, for causing her so much pain, for shattering her dreams of a future filled with laughter and sunshine.

"Mother," I said, my voice stronger this time, "you don't have to do that. Don't wear yourself out praying for me. It's okay."

"Don't you say that, child." Her voice was firm now, a steel thread running through it. "Don't you ever say that. Miracles happen. They do. And I won't stop praying until I see one for you."

I wanted to argue, to tell her that miracles were for fairy tales, for stories whispered in the dark, not for the harsh reality of our lives. But I couldn't. I saw the unwavering determination in her eyes, the fierce love that burned brighter than any candle, and I knew that arguing would be futile.

So I just closed my eyes, the dull ache behind my eyelids intensifying. The image of the Bible, of my mother's bowed head, of the silent, desperate prayers that filled the room, pressed in on me.

"I just want you to be well," she whispered, her voice thick with emotion. "I just want you to have a chance."

A chance. That was all I wanted too. A chance to experience the things that other girls my age took for granted and *more*. A chance to laugh, to dance, to fall in love, to simply live without the constant weight of constraints dragging me down.

But as I lay there, listening to my mother's soft breathing, feeling the warmth of her hand in mine, I couldn't shake the feeling that my chances were dwindling, fading like the light outside my window. My sixteenth birthday was approaching, a looming deadline, and I knew, deep in my heart, that even my mother's unwavering faith might not be enough to save me. The melancholic light of the room seemed to deepen, wrapping around me like a shroud, and I drifted back into the murky depths of sleep, haunted by the unspoken fears that hung between us, heavy and suffocating as the silence in the room. The birthday loomed, not as a celebration, but as a potential farewell.

14

The first thing I registered wasn't the sunlight filtering through the heavy velvet curtains, but the absence of pain. Usually, waking was a slow, arduous process, a climb out of a well of aches and stiffness. Today, though, there was only a quiet stillness, a lightness that felt almost... alien. I stretched, my limbs responding with a surprising ease. It was my sixteenth birthday. Sixteen. A milestone, they said. A turning point. But all I felt was a strange, unsettling calm.

I rose and went to the window, pulling back the curtains a fraction. The gardens, usually vibrant with color, seemed muted, almost gray, under the morning light. Our estate was vast, sprawling across acres of meticulously manicured lawns, ancient trees, and hidden fountains. It was beautiful, undeniably so, but it also felt like a gilded cage.

My family, or what remained of it, resided within its walls. My parents, perpetually lost in their own worlds of social obligations and quiet disappointments.

Today was supposed to be different. Sixteen was supposed to be... special. But as the day loomed closer, the familiar ache of loneliness had returned.The invitations had gone out weeks ago, elegant cards embossed with the family crest. The responses trickled back, polite but firm rejections, each one a tiny pinprick to my fragile hope. A prior engagement. An unavoidable business trip. A sudden illness. Always an excuse. I knew exactly why they refused to appear!

My parents, ever pragmatic, had decided on a smaller, more "intimate" gathering. They'd invited the gardeners, Mrs. Hawthorne and her son, Bartholomew, and the courtiers, a small, tight-knit group who had been with us for years. They were kind, in their own way, offering quiet smiles and words of encouragement when they saw me wandering the halls, lost in my own thoughts.

As I dressed, a simple gown of pale blue linen, a gift from Mrs. Hawthorne, a knot of sadness tightened in my chest. This wasn't how it was supposed to be. Birthdays were meant to be filled with laughter, with friends, with the overwhelming joy of being celebrated. Instead, it was just... quiet.

Downstairs, the dining room had been transformed. The long, imposing table, usually reserved for formal dinners, was draped with a cheerful floral tablecloth. Vases overflowing with wildflowers, undoubtedly gathered from the gardens, adorned the center. The air hummed with a gentle energy, a stark contrast to the usual sterile atmosphere.

Mrs. Hawthorne greeted me with a warm smile and a hug that felt surprisingly genuine. Bartholomew, a shy young man with kind eyes, offered a hesitant "Happy Birthday, Miss Orphia," his cheeks flushed. The courtiers, their faces creased with years of hard work and quiet wisdom, wished me well, their voices soft and melodic.

My parents arrived, their faces carefully composed. My mother wore a dress of shimmering silk, her hair perfectly coiffed. My father, as always, was impeccably dressed in a tailored suit. They wished me a happy birthday, their words polite but lacking warmth. They seemed more concerned with the arrangements, with ensuring that everything ran smoothly, than with actually celebrating with me.

The feast, though simple, was delicious. Mrs. Hawthorne had outdone herself, preparing a spread of roasted chicken, fresh vegetables, and crusty bread. There was even a small cake, decorated with sugared flowers, courtesy of the head cook. As we ate, a hesitant conversation flowed, punctuated by polite laughter and shared smiles.

I found myself drawn to Mrs. Hawthorne, her presence a comforting anchor in the sea of my own sadness. She told stories of the gardens, of the secrets whispered by the wind through the ancient trees, of the hidden creatures that dwelled within the overgrown thickets. Bartholomew, emboldened by his mother's presence, shared his dreams of becoming a sculptor, his eyes shining with passion.

The courtiers spoke of their families, of their hopes and dreams for their children. They were simple people, their lives far removed from the opulence of our estate, but their hearts were full of love and kindness.

As the afternoon wore on, a strange sense of peace settled over me. It wasn't the jubilant joy I had imagined, but a quiet acceptance, a gentle understanding. I realized that happiness wasn't necessarily about grand gestures or lavish celebrations. It was about connection, about finding solace in the company of those who truly cared.

My parents, after making a polite appearance, retreated to their studies, leaving me to enjoy the company of our staff. I didn't mind. In their absence, the room felt lighter, more authentic.

Later, as the sun began to set, casting long shadows across the lawn, I found myself sitting on the stone bench in the rose garden, a place I often sought refuge. The air was thick with the sweet scent of roses, their petals unfurling in the twilight.

Bartholomew joined me, his hands clasped in his lap. He didn't say anything, just sat beside me in comfortable silence. After a while, he reached into his pocket and pulled out a small, intricately carved wooden bird.

"I made this for you," he said, his voice barely a whisper. "I saw you watching the swallows in the courtyard, and I thought... well, I thought you might like it."

I took the bird from his hand, my fingers tracing the delicate carvings. It was a simple gift, but it held a depth of meaning that far surpassed any elaborate present. It was a symbol of connection, of understanding, of being seen. I was almost brought to tears.

"Thank you, Bartholomew," I said, my voice thick with emotion. "It's beautiful."

He smiled, a genuine, heartfelt smile that lit up his entire face. "Happy Birthday, Miss Orphia," he said.

As I sat there, holding the wooden bird in my hand, I realized that even in the midst of loneliness and disappointment, there was still beauty to be found. It wasn't the birthday I had envisioned, but it was a birthday filled with quiet kindness, with unexpected connections, with a gentle understanding that perhaps, just perhaps, I wasn't as alone as I thought. It was a melancholic celebration, bathed in the soft glow of the setting sun, but within that melancholy, a fragile seed of hope began to sprout. Perhaps sixteen wouldn't be so bad after all. Perhaps, in the quiet corners of my gilded cage, I could find my own version of happiness

15

The morning air hung heavy with the scent of damp earth and the promise of rain, a fitting aroma for the cloud that perpetually seemed to hover just above my head. Stepping out into the garden, the flagstones cool beneath my bare feet, I saw her. My mother. Perched on her usual wicker chair, the one with the faded floral cushions, she was a still life against the vibrant green canvas of the garden.

She was watching the birds, as she always did. Sparrows flitted amongst the branches of the ancient apple tree, their chirping a frantic, cheerful counterpoint to the quiet sorrow that permeated our days. I wondered what she saw in them, those tiny creatures, always in motion, always free. Perhaps she saw an escape. I knew I often did.

"Good morning," I said, my voice a little rough from sleep.

She didn't startle, didn't jump. She'd known I was there, I suppose. She always knew. She just turned her head slowly, a movement that seemed to take an enormous amount of energy, and offered a ghost of a smile.

"Good morning, little dove," she said, her voice raspy, like dried leaves rustling in the wind. "Did you sleep well?"

I shrugged, not wanting to lie, not wanting to burden her with the truth of my restless night. "Well enough."

She knew, of course. She always knew.

"And the birthday celebrations?" she asked, turning her gaze back to the frantic sparrows. "Did you enjoy them?"

The question felt like a pinprick to a balloon, deflating the carefully constructed image of joy I'd tried so hard to project the day before. The forced smiles of my parents, the awkward laughter, the well-meaning but ultimately hollow hugs. It had all felt like a performance, a charade enacted for her benefit, for the benefit of everyone who thought I should be moving on. I found joy in it but knew it foretold something worse coming ahead.

"Yes, I did," I said, the words tasting like ash in my mouth. "It was... nice."

Nice. Such a pathetic word to describe the anniversary of a day that had once held so much promise, so much unadulterated joy. A day that now served only as a stark reminder of what I had lost.

She was silent for a long moment, and I could feel her eyes on me, assessing, probing. She knew I was lying. She always knew.

The silence stretched, thick and suffocating, broken only by the chirping of the birds and the distant drone of a lawnmower. I shifted my weight, suddenly uncomfortable under her scrutiny. I wanted to tell her the truth, to confess the emptiness that had become my constant companion, but the words remained trapped in my throat, a heavy, indigestible lump.

Then, she did something unexpected. She stood up.

It was a laborious process, each movement stiff and deliberate, as if her joints were protesting the effort. She gripped the arms of the chair, her knuckles white, and pushed herself upright. For a moment, she swayed, her hand reaching out to steady herself. I instinctively moved forward, but she waved me away.

"I'm alright," she said, her voice stronger now, more urgent.

She stood there, ramrod straight, her frail frame somehow imbued with a sudden, unexpected power. She looked at me, really looked at me, her eyes, the same shade of blue as mine, piercing and intense.

And then she said it.

"Go," she said, her voice firm, unwavering. "Go now."

The word hung in the air between us, a single, sharp syllable that shattered the fragile peace of the morning. I stared at her, bewildered, unable to comprehend what she was saying.

"What?" I stammered, my voice barely a whisper.

She stepped closer, her hand reaching out to cup my face, her touch surprisingly strong. Her thumb traced the curve of my cheekbone, a gesture of love, of understanding.

"Go," she repeated, her voice softer now, but no less insistent. "Don't let me hold you back. You have to go."

Tears welled in my eyes, blurring her features. The garden seemed to tilt, the colors swirling together in a dizzying vortex.

"I don't understand," I choked out, the words a sob.

"Yes, you do," she said, her gaze unwavering. "You've been living in the shadows for too long. You've let it consume you. You can't stay here, with me, drowning in the past. You have to live. You have to find your own freedom."

"But what about you?" I asked the question in a desperate plea. "I can't just leave you. You need me."

She shook her head, a sad smile playing on her lips. "I'll be alright. I have my birds, my garden. And I have my memories. But you... you have a life to live. A future to create. Be free my child" , tears streamed down her pale face , her eyes bloodshot with irritation.

"But I don't want to," I said, the words tumbling out, raw and unfiltered. "I don't want to go."

The tears streamed down my face now, unchecked, unbidden. I clung to her hand, my grip desperate, pleading.

"I don't want to," I repeated, the words a mantra, a desperate attempt to ward off the inevitable. "I don't want to."

She looked at me, her eyes filled with a deep, profound sadness, but also with a fierce, unyielding love. She knew. She always knew. She knew that I was trapped, that I was suffocating, that I was slowly fading away. And she knew that the only way to save me was to push me away.

She squeezed my hand, her grip firm, reassuring.

"I know, little dove," she said, her voice barely audible above the chirping of the birds and the pounding of my heart. "I know. But you must. For yourself.."

And in that moment, standing there in the garden, the damp earth beneath my feet, the scent of rain in the air, I understood. I understood the depth of her love, the strength of her resolve. And I understood that she was right.

But I didn't want to go. I no longer had the energy for it. Perhaps, just perhaps, I could find a way to live.

16

The familiar drone of mumbled scripture dragged me from the depths of sleep, a heavy blanket woven with guilt and unease.

"Be kind and compassionate to one another, forgiving each other, just as in Christ God forgave you."

"If we confess our sins, he is faithful and just and will forgive us our sins and purify us from all unrighteousness."

"I will give them an undivided heart and put a new spirit in them; I will remove from them their heart of stone and give them a heart of flesh."

My eyelids fluttered open, and the first thing I saw was her face, hovering above me like a pale moon. The harsh morning light etched the lines around her mouth deeper, highlighting the insecurity and fear that was her constant companion.

"Mother," I croaked, my throat thick with the residue of troubled dreams.

She didn't respond, didn't even acknowledge that I was awake, continuing her hushed reading from the worn leather-bound Bible clutched in her hands. The verses felt like accusations, each syllable a pointed finger reminding me of my transgressions. I knew her actions to be of good intentions , but I also knew how she viewed me 'A sinner' that she so desperately wanted to be forgiven.

The air in the room was thick with the scent of dust and dried lavender, a scent I usually found comforting, but now, it felt suffocating, another layer in the oppressive atmosphere she created. I shifted in the bed, trying to break free from the invisible chains of her presence.

Finally, she lowered the book, her gaze, sharper than any blade, fixing on me. "So child , tell me , what did you do those days you fled from us so cruelly?"

It wasn't a question. It was a pronouncement, a judgment delivered from the pulpit of our shared history.

Before I could formulate a response, before I could even fully gather my bearings, she lunged, her hand snaking out and clamping around my arm with surprising strength. A jolt of pain shot through me, radiating from the pressure of her grip.

"Tell me," she hissed, her voice low and dangerous. "Tell me exactly what you did."

My breath hitched in my throat. "Did?" I stammered, trying to pull away, but her grip tightened, the bones in my arm protesting.

"When you ran away," she spat the words like venom. "When you abandoned your family, shamed us all. What did you do? Where did you go?"

Panic began to bubble inside me. I had known this confrontation was inevitable, had rehearsed countless scenarios in my head during my brief escape, but none of them had prepared me for the sheer force of her fury.

"I... I went to the village," I managed, the words tumbling out in a rush. "I walked in the forest."

Her eyes narrowed further, boring into me with an intensity that made me want to shrink back into the pillows. "Lies," she breathed. "Don't lie to me. I can see it in your eyes. What did you do in the forest? Who did you meet?"

"No one," I insisted, my voice trembling. "I didn't meet anyone. I just... I just needed to be alone."

"Alone?" She laughed, a harsh, grating sound that sent shivers down my spine. "Alone with your sins, no doubt. Tell me the truth! I deserve to know the truth!"

Her grip tightened again, and I cried out in pain. The room swam, the floral wallpaper blurring into a kaleidoscope of dizzying patterns. I was trapped, pinned beneath the weight of her accusations, suffocating in the suffocating atmosphere of our shared past.

"I told you," I pleaded, tears welling in my eyes. "I didn't do anything. I just walked. I needed to think."

But she wasn't listening. She was lost in her own world of righteous indignation, convinced of my inherent wickedness. Her face was contorted with rage, spittle flecking the corners of her mouth.

"You think you can just run away and come back as if nothing happened?" she screamed, her voice cracking with emotion. "You think you can just shame us like that and expect swift forgiveness? You'll tell me what you did! You'll confess your sins!"

She shook my arm violently, and I felt a searing pain in my shoulder. My vision narrowed, focusing on the burning pressure of her fingers digging into my flesh. I was a trapped animal, desperate for escape.

My gaze darted around the room, searching for a lifeline, for anything that could break this suffocating hold. My eyes landed on the small porcelain vase on the bedside table, a delicate thing filled with dried flowers, a relic from a happier time, a time I barely remembered.

In a surge of desperate energy, fueled by fear and a lifetime of pent-up resentment, I lunged for it. My fingers closed around the cool, smooth surface of the vase, and without a second thought, I swung it with all my might.

The vase connected with her face with a sickening thud. The porcelain shattered, sending shards flying through the air like deadly confetti. The dried flowers scattered across the bed, their fragile petals wilting against the harsh reality of violence.

For a moment, there was only silence, a ringing emptiness that filled the room. My mother staggered back, her hand flying to her face. Her eyes, wide with disbelief and pain, stared at me, uncomprehending. A thin trickle of blood snaked down her cheek, staining the collar of her worn cotton dress.

I stared back at her, my heart pounding in my chest, my breath coming in ragged gasps. The vase lay in pieces at my feet, a symbol of something broken, something irreparable. The air hung heavy with the scent of shattered porcelain and spilled blood.

Then, a low moan escaped her lips, followed by a torrent of tears. She sank to her knees, her body shaking with sobs. The sound was raw and guttural, a primal expression of pain that cut through me like a knife.

I stood frozen, the adrenaline slowly receding, leaving me weak and trembling. What had I done? I had crossed a line, a boundary I never thought I was capable of crossing.

The silence stretched, thick and suffocating. The weight of what I had done pressed down on me, crushing me beneath its immensity. I had silenced her, but in doing so, I had also silenced something within myself.

The melancholic drone of scripture was replaced by the raw, unfiltered sound of her grief, and in that moment, I didn't know which was more unbearable. The escape I had so desperately craved had led me here, to this shattered space, to this unbearable silence, to this profound and irreversible act. And the truth, the horrifying, undeniable truth, was that I had no idea what to do next. The forest, the village, the escape , all of it had led to this. A broken vase, a broken bond, and a future irrevocably stained with the color of blood.

I had never committed such an act of violence before. What had come over me? What had changed me so deeply that I would attack and maim my own mother?

Tears fell from my eyes like a waterfall , I sat up reaching my arms out towards her. "Mother , mother , I didn't mean to!" , instead of punishing me , striking me back , she fell to her knees in front of me , embracing my legs tightly. I could feel her blood and tears pierce through my nightdress a mixture of cool and warm liquid.

"You are my only child , my only daughter , why does God have to test us so cruelly , is it I that did this to us both?"

Words darted through my head as I heard my mother's desperate pleas for stability. Though I could not bring myself to speak a single one of them , my throat was

swollen with grief , my breath horse , my eyes bloodshot and burning. The words were trapped cruelly in the back of my throat.

17

Throughout those days after my sixteenth birthday I walked around the house in deep thought , a great uncertainty weighing on me like a paperweight. Had I completely separated myself from society with my behaviour? Would I ever be able to marry and have my own children? If I could not , what would come of my life? What would I do? What shall become of me?

****

And you , my dear reader, must be waiting with the utmost patience to know. Did my nightmare and the fear that came with it become true. Did I live a life short lived?

Orphia ~

Yes.

I died at the age of sixteen in the very bed that my prophetic nightmare transpired , in childbirth. Neither myself nor my child survived the ordeal.

My father thought me deserving of it , my sins and debaucherous behaviour disgusted his god fearing beliefs and lifestyle. Though truthfully I never knew my actions to ever be sins. I did not even know that my actions would result in the creation of a child.

I spit upon you father! You and the false , cruel , unworthy God that you and many others worship! God cannot be found in books or 'holy places' *she* is not made by man , *she* creates man!

My mother, on the other hand , would not allow my body to be taken from my bed for over 5 days. She screamed and attacked any who entered to try and steal my and my child's corpses. I wanted to hold her and tell her *'Mother my pain is over'* , but for days I was still trapped inside myself, unable to move in the cocoon of my own cold flesh , with my deceased daughter still between my bloodied legs , I could not even see , for my eyes where closed shut , I could only hear the cries and screams of my mother's grief and my father's cruel commanding voice attempting to remove it with fear and violence. My father was glad that myself and my child were deceased , he refused to call for a doctor or midwife when my labor had begun , sealing our fate. No longer a burden to him and his high social status.

My mother had always told me that if I were to have a granddaughter she would have liked her to be named Agnes , it was customary in my family for grandparents to name grandchildren and so that is my daughter's name, though she will never know it.

My soul was only able to escape my body before my funeral. After the 5 days had ceased and my mother's grief had drained every ounce of energy from her body, she had nothing left inside her , they were finally able to remove my body from my bed , my room and then the house. As soon as they opened the door I fell out of their arms landing on the cold stone floor , my daughter landed next to me , her innocent cries filling my ears , I wondered how those around could not hear them. I pulled down my nightgown gently from my collarbone and instinctively took her to my breast , she latched on and suckled greedily, for most newborns their first taste of milk is what gives them life , this was Agnes's first taste of death , this was barbaric , she shall suckle from me forever , cruelly stuck in the body of an infant for all eternity.

I was told about stories of '*The Grim Reaper*' , he who is death that comes to take you to the other side , dressed in a long black cloak with a gaunt white face. I was not greeted by such a figure , I was quite displeased.

My funeral was nothing like my nightmare , it was not held in a church or cemetery , me and my child were buried together in the ground surrounding the house , a stone was erected but my daughter's existence was not acknowledged on it , the cold grey stone simply only held my name , that was all , no reasoning for my death.

My mother , my sweet mother , she visited my grave every morning until she too died. There were two other visitors in the dark night , *Elijah* and *Beryl* , my two lovers. I was brought to tears at the very sight of them , I truly thought that I would never see them again. They laid down the most colourful flowers from the forest that they could find , and asked for my forgiveness, their green eyes looking up towards the sky as they spoke , their lips trembling with guilt , I wish I could have assured them that I loved them very dearly, that they did me no wrong , that I longed to be held by them again , to feel their lips press against my skin , to feel the heat radiating from their bodies, to be entangled in lovers embrace. But the only thing I could do was watch with love and horror. If I reached out to touch them , I would only slip through them. I was no longer a part of the world that houses the living.

But even so I was content in my ability to watch the lives of the living without having to take part in it. I am able to view all the different types of life that live on after me. I can see the birds rearing their small hairless offspring into creatures of feathered beauty. I am to see the birth and creation of other human beings and the animals that they share the land of the living with. I watch with patience to see how the world and society continue to change.

And as I have watched the tableau of the world change colour and texture , I have realised one thing , as humans we long to escape suffering , we do not want to feel pain , but without it our lives have little meaning , we are almost no longer human , there is no meaning for our existence. Without my melancholy , I would perhaps have lived a much longer life , but I would have been trapped inside my own flesh rotting from the inside , a life not worth living . The fact that we feel pleasure *and* pain is exactly what makes us human beings.

~ *Orphia*

ACKNOWLEDGEMENTS:

~The artwork displayed on the cover ~ *Fatima Ronquillo*

~ The artworks displayed on pages 33 , 36 , 39 ~ *The Malleus Maleficarum by Heinrich Kramer*

~ The books watermark ~ *'Jacob Bryant's Orphic Egg (1774)'*

Printed in Dunstable, United Kingdom

64322496R00109